JUSTICE LEAGUE UNLIMITED

BATMAN™
JUSTICE FOR ALL

written by John Sazaklis
designed by Can2 Design Group
Batman created by Bob Kane

D0822749

studio fun

A READER'S DIGEST COMPANY

White Plains, New York • Montréal, Québec • Bath, United Kingdom

Nightfall has covered the gleaming bright city of Metropolis like a heavy blanket. High above the skyline stands the LexCorp building. It is the home and office of Lex Luthor. Not only is Lex Luthor the wealthiest and most brilliant man in Metropolis, he is also one of its most dangerous.

Superman protects the city of Metropolis from people like Lex Luthor. On this particular night, the Man of Steel had been investigating the trading of illegal weapons throughout the country and all the clues led him directly to Luthor. Superman pays Lex Luthor an unexpected after-hours visit.

SO THIS IS HOW IT ENDS, SUPERMAN. I'VE CARRIED THIS AROUND FOR YEARS WAITING FOR JUST THE RIGHT MOMENT. ANY LAST REQUESTS?

JUST TELL ME ONE THING. HOW DID YOU GET ALL THOSE WEAPONS THROUGH CUSTOMS?

Upon entering the billionaire's private penthouse, Superman is welcomed by Luthor with a very peculiar gift—Kryptonite! Its green glow washes over the Man of Steel, knocking him to the floor. Lex laughs at the misfortune of his fallen foe.

EASY. WHEN MONEY TALKS, PEOPLE LISTEN. I BRIBED MANY BUSINESSMEN TO TAKE CARE OF MY BUSINESS.

SO YOU'LL HAVE PLENTY OF COMPANY IN PRISON.

I DON'T THINK SO, SUPERMAN. MY CRIMES, LIKE YOU, ARE ABOUT TO BE HISTORY!

Immediately after Lex Luthor's confession, Superman springs back to his feet. The bald billionaire is in shock.

Suddenly, the blue-and-red clad form of Superman changes before Luthor's eyes, morphing into that of the green-skinned Martian Manhunter!

WHAT?! BUT THE KRYPTONITE...

IS USELESS AGAINST ME.

Seconds later, the office door bursts off its hinges. The room is bathed with more glowing green light. It is emanating from Green Lantern's power ring. The Galactic Guardian hovers in the air while Batman, the Caped Crusader, stands by his side. Luthor regards the heroes with contempt and rage.

NO! I'VE BEEN SET UP!

AND NOW YOU'RE GOING DOWN!

Green Lantern confiscates the radioactive rock from Luthor's possession with a beam of hard light energy. Batman takes it and places it in a special lead-lined compartment in his Utility Belt.

MISSION ACCOMPLISHED.

Lex holds up a remote-control switch and activates it. The penthouse begins to rumble as a high-tech jet appears outside the window. The plane's mounted cannon takes aim at the heroes and fires red-hot laser beams through the glass. Batman, Martian Manhunter, and Green Lantern duck for cover.

BEEP!

THE ONLY THING YOU ACCOMPLISHED IS YOUR DEMISE, BATMAN!

CHOOM!

Before John Stewart, Hal Jordan and Guy Gardner protected Earth.

Luthor leaps out of the broken window and climbs into the aircraft. Then he fires three missiles at the super heroes. The explosives detonate upon impact!

LEX LUTHOR ALWAYS BRINGS DOWN THE HOUSE!

BOOM! BOOM! BOOM!

Luthor's penthouse collapses into a heap of smoldering rubble, burying Batman, Martian Manhunter, and Green Lantern. When the smoke clears, the heroes emerge, safely protected inside Green Lantern's force field.

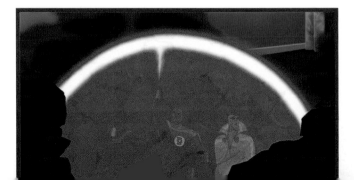

WHOOSH!

The criminal mastermind cackles with glee. He savors his victory as he zooms away over the Metropolis skyline.

All of a sudden, a red and blue blur streaks against the night sky–it is Superman! The Man of Steel is in hot pursuit of the escaping evildoer. Spying Superman on his tail, Luthor lets loose a volley of powerful rockets. One of them is a direct hit and it stuns the hero.

KA-BOOM!

THIS TIME I TOOK DOWN THE REAL SUPERMAN!

Luthor laughs a maniacal laugh at his good luck but it does not last long. The billionaire suddenly doubles over in pain. He loses control and the aircraft careens in between buildings.

Superman recovers just in time to rush to the rescue. He catches Luthor's flying vehicle and brings it in for a safe landing. Superman rips open the cockpit with his bare hands, ready to reprimand the bald businessman, but stops in surprise. Lex Luthor is almost lifeless inside!

Moments later, Lex Luthor wakes up in a hospital bed with Superman and Dr. Patel standing by his side. Their expressions are grim, but Luthor is boiling with rage.

> YOU CAN'T HOLD ME IN HERE. I'LL GET THE BEST LAWYERS AND–

> LEX, THIS IS SERIOUS. YOU HAD A SEIZURE.

> MY RESEARCH SHOWS THAT YOUR PROLONGED EXPOSURE TO KRYPTONITE HAS GIVEN YOU A RARE FORM OF BLOOD POISONING.

> WHAT?!
> THIS IS YOUR FAULT, SUPERMAN!! YOU'LL PAY FOR THIS!

Luthor is even more furious. He snatches the chart from the doctor and verifies his condition. It is true. The Kryptonite has made him sick. He hurls the chart in disgust at Superman. It bounces harmlessly off the Man of Steel and papers scatter all over the floor.

After his medical examination, Lex Luthor is escorted to a high-security prison. His cell is sparse and drab, with only the bare necessities. The uniform provided by the guards is also cheap and uncomfortable. This is a far cry from Luthor's luxurious lifestyle.

Still angry after the events of the day, Luthor tries to quiet his mind and get some sleep. As he drifts off to dreamland, he is awakened by music blaring from the cell next door.

Luthor tries to drown out the sound by pressing the pillow against his ears. Frustrated, he gets up and pounds against the wall, demanding peace and quiet, but his cries go unheeded.

Using his extreme intelligence, Lex breaks into the TV cable box and devises a way to hack into the neighbor's video feed. He discovers that his neighbor is none other than Ultra-Humanite— genius, madman, and giant albino ape.

HUMANITE! HOW CAN YOU STAND THAT CATERWAULING?

IT'S CLASSICAL OPERA. YOU SHOULD TRY IT. IT COULD IMPROVE YOUR DISPOSITION.

A LITTLE FREEDOM WOULD IMPROVE IT JUST FINE. I NEED YOUR HELP AND I'M WILLING TO PAY.

I'M LISTENING.

Scientist Gerard Shugel's body was stricken with disease, so he discovered how to transfer his brain into other bodies and became Ultra-Humanite.

In addition to his great intellect and refined tastes, Ultra-Humanite is inhumanly strong.

11

Unlike most other primates, gorillas spend very little time in trees, although they are skillful climbers.

Adult male gorillas in the wild weigh between 300 and 400 pounds.

Luthor recruits Ultra-Humanite to help him escape, promising him an exorbitant amount of money. Humanite is intrigued and more than willing to exercise his brain with such an interesting challenge. He gets to work immediately, disassembling the insides of his TV set, creating a crafty means of escape.

That night, when the guards come to deliver his dinner, Ultra-Humanite pretends he is too weak to retrieve it himself. He asks the guards kindly to lay it on the table in his cell. The guards take precaution and arm themselves. Before they can reach the albino ape, the guards step onto an electric shock pad hidden under the rug!

WHAT A *SHOCKING* SURPRISE!

Ultra-Humanite quickly finds the guards' access pass and uses it to open Luthor's cell. Then the diabolical duo makes their way out of the prison. They do not get very far before an alarm blares. Guards in the watchtower shine the spotlight down on Luthor and Ultra-Humanite.

Luthor follows Humanite's orders. The agile ape leaps off the roof of the prison and climbs nimbly up the fence. The guards fire their laser pistols at the fugitives, but to no avail. In the blink of an eye, Lex Luthor and Ultra-Humanite disappear into the night.

Meanwhile, Batman patrols the streets of Metropolis in his sleek armored vehicle, the Batmobile. The Dark Knight is listening to the police scanner and a special bulletin is broadcast.

"LEX LUTHOR AND ULTRA-HUMANITE HAVE ESCAPED AND ARE CONSIDERED ARMED AND DANGEROUS."

SCREE!

Batman slams on the brakes. The Batmobile's tires squeal and he burns rubber. Batman turns the wheel and drives back toward the prison.

At the same time, Luthor and Humanite are running down the streets when they hear the familiar sound of the Batmobile. The perfidious pair run into a dark alley and hide behind a dumpster.

Luthor reveals a package of explosives he had hidden on his person. He throws it into a nearby building. An earsplitting explosion rocks the foundation and the building bursts into flames. Batman changes course and charges toward the blaze. He assesses the situation. There are people in danger and not a moment to lose. The Caped Crusader contacts the Justice League.

The Batmobile has many features—including bulletproof glass, ejector seats, and a smoke screen dispenser.

The Batmobile even has an armored stationary mode to prevent people from tampering with the car when it is left unattended.

Batman looks up to see a little girl screaming in the window. He pulls out his grappling hook and aims it at the roof. Quick as a flash, the Dark Knight is hoisted up into the air and somersaults into the burning building.

HELP ME, I'M SCARED.

Batman scoops the child up and carefully wraps her in his fireproof cape. Then he sprints for the window. SMASH! Fractured wooden beams land before them. With his path blocked by falling debris, Batman must find another exit. He kicks open the door and runs for the stairs.

Suddenly, the stairs crumble and collapse. Batman is trapped with no way out! Just as the floor gives way, a winged figure swoops down and grabs Batman in the nick of time.

WHOOSH!

It is the Thanagarian warrior–Hawkgirl! She
flies high over the inferno as the flames lick at
her feet. Once they are clear of the blaze,
Hawkgirl and Batman land on the street.
Relieved, the little girl runs into the arms of her
father. The police escort the remaining
residents out of the building while the
firefighters hose down the blaze. The Flash and
Superman aid the rescue teams as Batman
regards Hawkgirl silently.

I'M USED TO
BEING THANKED
WHEN I SAVE
SOMEONE.

I'M NOT
USED TO
BEING SAVED.

BAD NEWS.
I'VE LOST
THE TRAIL OF
LUTHOR AND
HUMANITE.

NO BIGGIE.
THEY'RE
JUST TWO
GUYS.
HOW MUCH
TROUBLE
CAN THEY
BE?

The next day, the feline felon known as Cheetah slinks cautiously inside an abandoned novelty toy factory. She is responding to an anonymous phone call for a very profitable job. Suddenly, a shadow slithers up behind her. It is Copperhead—the slinky, sleazy assassin.

I HEAR WE'LL BE WORKING CLOSELY TOGETHER.

UGH! I WOULDN'T TOUCH YOU TO SCRATCH YOU.

Cheetah was once a genetic research scientist who tested her theories on herself. She turned to crime when her funding ran out.

Copperhead sticks out his tongue at Cheetah. She backs away and bumps into Solomon Grundy—the living zombie! The simpleminded monster strokes Cheetah's furry shoulder.

NICE KITTY!

SLASH!

Cheetah bares her claws and scratches him. The angry zombie attacks back, punching a crate and smashing it to smithereens. Copperhead jumps onto the brute's back and grabs him in a headlock.

Suddenly, the room plunges into darkness. This is the work of the shadow-manipulating villain known as the Shade.

HEY, WHO TURNED OUT THE LIGHTS?

I DID. AND I'LL DO WORSE IF YOU KEEP ACTING LIKE UNRULY CHILDREN.

Star Sapphire's alien gemstone gives her the ability to fly and manipulate powerful energy beams.

Star Sapphire descends from above. The intergalactic villainess is not pleased with the arrangements.

SO, MY COHORTS ARE SIMPLE COMMON CRIMINALS.

Lex Luthor and Ultra-Humanite enter the room. Luthor greets his guests with uncharacteristic kindness.

CRIMINALS, YES. BUT NOT COMMON! GLAD YOU COULD MAKE IT.

CUT THE COURTESIES. WHY DID YOU INVITE US HERE?

I HAVE NEED OF YOUR UNIQUE SERVICES. YOU WILL ALL BE PAID HANDSOMELY IF YOU CAN DO ONE SIMPLE JOB. DESTROY THE JUSTICE LEAGUE!

The Watchtower is the orbiting space base of the Justice League.

Far, far away in the expanse of space, Batman, Hawkgirl, and The Flash are on the main deck of the Watchtower. Batman is monitoring the computer, waiting for their foes to strike again. The newscaster reports that the dangerous culprit is none other than Ultra-Humanite! Batman regards The Flash very sternly.

NO BIGGIE, HUH?

IT WAS JUST A JOKE!

YOU KNOW HOW HE FEELS ABOUT JOKES, RIGHT?

Meanwhile, the Metropolis police force has barricaded the building. The head officer tries to negotiate with the great albino ape.

HUMANITE! LET THE HOSTAGE GO AND I'LL GIVE YOU ONE OF MY MEN IN RETURN.

WHAT DO YOU TAKE ME FOR, A TROGLODYTE? NO DEAL!

Martian Manhunter often stands guard at the Watchtower as its primary sentry.

22

Superman zooms through the air and slams into Ultra-Humanite with a double-fisted punch.

The first man-made satellite, Sputnik 1, was launched into space by Russia in 1957.

KA-POW!

The villain loses his grip on the hostage. Batman drops down stealthily from the roof and rushes to her side. He tells Green Lantern to go inside the building and search for more hostages.

YOU'RE SAFE NOW.

BUT YOU'RE NOT!

"Troglodyte" is an insulting term for a person regarded as intentionally ignorant or old-fashioned.

The hostage reveals herself to be the Cheetah in disguise! She slashes at Batman but he nimbly leaps out of reach. The Cheetah's razor-sharp claws slice through his cape. Batman realizes that Ultra-Humanite lured the Justice League to the federal building deliberately.

LOOKS LIKE THE CAT'S OUT OF THE BAG!

IT'S A TRAP!

FELINES AND REPTILES LIKE TO PREY ON RODENTS, BATMAN!

BATS ARE NOT RODENTS.

Copperhead sneaks up behind Batman and tries to take a bite out of the crime fighter. The Dark Knight deftly throws Copperhead over his shoulder right into the oncoming Cheetah.

The villains tumble, but are back on their feet to face off against Batman together.

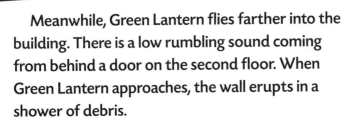

Meanwhile, Green Lantern flies farther into the building. There is a low rumbling sound coming from behind a door on the second floor. When Green Lantern approaches, the wall erupts in a shower of debris.

Solomon Grundy bursts out from behind, catching the hero off guard. Green Lantern wills his power ring to lift him into the air but Grundy grabs him by the ankle. The zombie slams Green Lantern through the floor and into the lobby.

Before Green Lantern can recover, Solomon Grundy drops on top of him through the hole in the ceiling. Then he pummels the hero with his fists of fury.

WHAP!
WHAP!
WHAP!
WHAP!

HEY UGLY, MEET MY MACE!

SMACK!

In an instant, Hawkgirl comes crashing through a window, brandishing her weapon. It crackles with electric energy. She knocks Solomon Grundy clear across the room into a column. The pillar topples and crushes Grundy underneath.

Just as suddenly, The Flash rushes to Batman's side and punches out Copperhead while Wonder Woman lassos the Cheetah. She hoists the villainess into the air.

HANG TIGHT.

LOOKS LIKE WE EVENED THE ODDS!

THAT'S WHAT YOU THINK. SAY GOOD NIGHT, SMILEY!

Out from the shadows emerges the Shade to tip the scales in the Injustice League's favor. The morose manipulator traps The Flash in a bubble of darkness, and hurls him into a wall.

Then he aims his staff at Hawkgirl and cloaks her in a sticky shadow.

The Shade gloats with a laugh but his victory is short-lived. Batman rushes at the villain and delivers a devastating kick that knocks the Shade out of the fight.

WHAM!

IF ANYONE CAN LIGHT UP A ROOM, IT'S ME!

ZZZARK!

IT'S LIGHTS OUT FOR YOU, TOO.

Star Sapphire attacks Batman with her magic gem. A beam of energy streaks past the hero's head. Batman evades the blasts long enough to produce his trusty Batarang. He hurls it at the villainess with expert accuracy, hitting her crown.

Star Sapphire's next shot goes wide and incinerates a girder overhead.

The heavy structure collapses. Wonder Woman drops the Cheetah and rushes to the rescue. She catches the girder with her Amazonian strength. Star Sapphire then fires her cosmic rays at Wonder Woman, who deflects them with her unbreakable silver bracelets.

Wonder Woman's lariat is also known as the Golden Lasso of Truth. Whomever she ensnares with it is compelled to tell the truth.

At the other end of the lobby, Superman continues his fight with Ultra-Humanite. The two titans clash and trade blows. The Man of Steel punches Humanite across the room. Then he uses his super-speed to quickly grip the gorilla in a headlock.

Superman's super-hearing picks up an extra heartbeat. He looks up to see Lex Luthor watching the melee like a spectator at a sporting event.

SO YOU'RE BEHIND ALL THIS, LUTHOR!

I AM, AND MY TEAM IS BETTER THAN YOURS! NOW COME ON, HUMANITE! PUT YOUR BACK INTO IT.

Heeding Luthor's advice, Humanite springs backward, crunching Superman against the wall. SPLAT! The Man of Steel is momentarily dazed. Humanite seizes the opportunity and throws Superman into a column.

BASH!

THUD!

THE FRIEND OF MY ENEMY IS STILL MY ENEMY.

Using his grappling hook, Batman swings onto the upper level and confronts Lex Luthor. The malicious mastermind quickly draws his weapon from its holster but the Dark Knight moves faster. He tackles Luthor to the ground. Batman slaps the weapon away and Luthor head-butts Batman in return before retrieving his weapon.

Copperhead takes his name from venomous snakes in the pit viper family. Their bites are rarely fatal.

Wonder Woman sees Batman trapped in Luthor's sights but cannot reach him because she is still under attack from Star Sapphire's barrage of energy blasts. Thinking quickly, the Amazon deflects one of the cosmic rays, aiming it directly at Luthor. The energy beam ricochets off the balcony, blowing it to bits.

While Batman gets to his feet, a slithering shape sneaks up behind him. Copperhead makes his move and sinks his fangs into Batman! The Dark Knight winces from the pain.

Suddenly, a blinding beam of green light jettisons the scaly scoundrel into the far wall.

The Shade has many dark powers, including teleportation.

With the tide turning against the Injustice League, Luthor commands his cohorts to retreat. The Shade covers the whole building and its surroundings in shadow and absconds with his team. Green Lantern eliminates the cloak of darkness with a light burst from his ring.

Left behind are an unconscious Copperhead— and a poisoned Batman!

Teleportation is moving instantly from one place to another without traveling the physical space between them.

The Justice League rushes back to the Watchtower so Batman can get medical attention. A short while later, the Dark Knight wakes up to find Superman and Martian Manhunter looming over him.

THE VENOM ANTIDOTE IS WORKING.

WELCOME BACK. WE THOUGHT WE LOST YOU.

Batman does not like that idea. He waits for Superman to leave and then gets out of bed. Martian Manhunter tells Batman that, as the only member of the League without superpowers, it is best that he take enough time to recuperate. Batman has made up his mind.

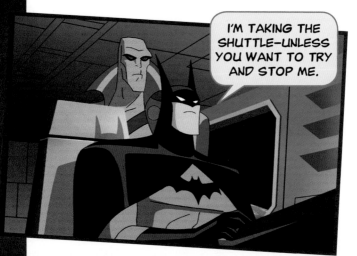

I'M TAKING THE SHUTTLE—UNLESS YOU WANT TO TRY AND STOP ME.

Meanwhile, Superman and The Flash head down to Stryker's Island maximum-security prison. They visit Copperhead in custody and attempt to interrogate the villain.

TELL US WHERE LUTHOR IS!

I DON'T KNOW ANYTHING. I'M JUST AN INNOCENT VICTIM OF CIRCUMSTANCE.

WE'VE HEARD THAT BEFORE. TELL US ANOTHER.

The scaly scoundrel enjoys teasing the super heroes. This frustrates Superman, and the Man of Steel loses his cool. He grabs Copperhead and lifts him off the ground.

I'M WARNING YOU.

HOW DOES BATMAN DO IT?

OOH, IS THE BIG BLUE BOY SCOUT GONNA MAKE ME SPILL MY GUTS? I DON'T THINK SO.

MUST BE THE MASK.

Disgusted, Superman drops Copperhead and calls for the guards. As they escort him back to his cell, the prisoner sticks his tongue out at the heroes.

Back at the abandoned warehouse, Lex Luthor berates the Injustice League for their failed attempt at destroying the Justice League.

WHAT WAS I THINKING? THAT WAS PATHETIC!

YOU GOT WHAT YOU PAID FOR.

ARE YOU SAYING YOU WANT MORE MONEY? YOU WANT TO BE REWARDED FOR FAILURE? FORGET IT!

The other members of the team argue with their employer. Amidst the shouting and cursing, Solomon Grundy grabs Luthor by the neck and threatens him.

GIVE US MONEY, OR GRUNDY CRUSH YOU.

GO AHEAD. I'M ALREADY A DEAD MAN. JUST LIKE YOU.

The living zombie regards his leader for a
moment and releases him. Finally, the Cheetah
says what everyone is thinking.

YOU'RE CRAZY.

Suddenly, the main doors to the factory burst
open. A pointy-haired silhouette stands in the
frame. Laughing maniacally, he steps into the light.
It is the Joker!

WHAT'S WRONG WITH
CRAZY? IT'S DONE
WONDERS FOR ME!
HA HA HA HA!

The Joker prances through the room, greeting everyone with his signature sinister grin. He puts on a festive hat and pulls out an air horn. Luthor sneers at the uninvited guest.

Grundy obeys his orders and reaches for the Joker. The criminal clown gasses the big brute with the trick air horn. A cloud of sleeping gas immediately incapacitates Grundy. He falls down face-first and is fast asleep in seconds.

The Joker plucks an undetected tracer from Luthor's shoulder. The other villains gasp in surprise. It had been placed there during Luthor's brief struggle with Batman at the federal building. Fuming that he was foiled by the cleverness of the Caped Crusader, Luthor suspects that Batman is most certainly on his way to their location!

The Joker's bizarre array of weapons includes flowers that shoot acid and oversized mallets.

SERIOUSLY, LEX. YOU NEED ME.

I NEED YOU LIKE I NEED A SKIN RASH.

MAYBE SO, BUT I KNOW SOMETHING YOU DON'T KNOW. I KNOW HOW THE BAT THINKS!

Batman has locked the Joker away in Arkham Asylum countless times, but the Joker always seems to find a way to escape.

Moments later, the Dark Knight lands on the roof of the abandoned toy factory. He picks open the skylight with a miniature tool set from his Utility Belt. Silently and stealthily, he climbs down on his Batrope. The blipping signal on his locator increases its frequency as Batman approaches the end of the second-floor landing.

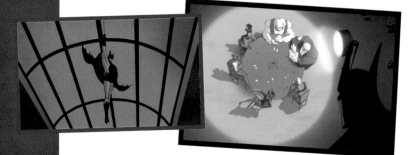

Directly below him, the crime fighter finds the Injustice League gathered around a table playing cards. Preparing to strike the sitting ducks, Batman does not notice his arch nemesis sneak up behind him with a bowling ball bag. The Joker hits Batman on the head, sending him over the railing and onto the table below.

The Joker is also known as the Clown Prince of Crime. His real identity has never been revealed.

CRASH!

The Injustice League stares at the fallen form of Batman, dumbstruck at their luck. The Joker cackles with maniacal glee. The Dark Knight is now their prisoner!

THE CLOWN'S TRAP ACTUALLY WORKED.

HA! HA! HA! HA! HA! HA! HA!

A "strike" is a term used in bowling to indicate that all pins have been knocked down with the first ball of a frame.

41

Titanium is a chemical element with the symbol Ti. It is known for its silver color, low density, and high strength.

When Batman comes to, he finds himself tightly bound in a stasis pod. His Utility Belt has been removed and he is surrounded by the Injustice League.

The villains argue about keeping Batman alive. Luthor explains that the Dark Knight's restraints are made of pure titanium and that the stasis field around him will block out any telepathy, thus preventing Martian Manhunter from locating his teammate. Then he turns his attention back to Batman.

Martian Manhunter's telepathy allows the team to stay in contact across vast distances.

Solomon Grundy attempts to open the
Caped Crusader's Utility Belt, but he is zapped
by a high-voltage electric current.

Batman's
Utility Belt
contains most
of his tools,
including his
Batarangs.
It is booby-
trapped to
prevent
tampering.

Luthor takes the belt. He orders his biggest
brawlers, Ultra-Humanite and Solomon
Grundy, to guard Batman.

Deep underground, Lex Luthor has created a makeshift laboratory for his scientific research. He tries to analyze the Utility Belt with an X-ray but the belt's high-tech security features make it impenetrable. The belt short-circuits the X-ray and the machine explodes.

FASCINATING.

CAREFUL! JUST BECAUSE YOU WON'T LIVE TO SEE OLD AGE DOESN'T MEAN THE REST OF US DON'T WANT TO!

KA-BOOM!

Meanwhile, the Dark Knight wastes no time using his wits to turn Solomon Grundy and Humanite against each other.

GRUNDY, WHAT'S LUTHOR PAYING YOU FOR THIS?

AS MUCH AS ME? DON'T BE PREPOSTEROUS.

MONEY. LOTS OF IT.

AS MUCH AS HIM?

LOOK AT WHAT HAPPENED TO YOU, GRUNDY. DO YOU THINK IT'S FAIR?

The two titans tumble and tussle. Solomon Grundy grabs Ultra-Humanite in a headlock and pounds his fist into the gorilla's oversized brain.

GRRR! GRUNDY MAD AT MONKEY!

WHAP!

GET YOUR HANDS OFF ME, YOU WORTHLESS ZOMBIE!

Upstairs, the entire structure rumbles, distracting Luthor from his experiments on the belt. He rushes out of the lab toward Batman's holding cell. There, he finds Solomon Grundy and Ultra-Humanite locked in battle. Luthor sighs and holds his head in his hand. Then he screams at his two henchmen.

YOU IMBECILES ARE KILLING ME FASTER THAN THE KRYPTONITE!

Annoyed, Luthor assigns the Cheetah to watch Batman instead while he returns to his lab. The villainess hisses and extends her claws.

The first woman to call herself Cheetah debuted in *Wonder Woman* #6 in October 1943.

In the lab, Lex Luthor turns his attention to Batman's Utility Belt. The evil genius is making progress when the Joker bursts into the room.

CHEETAH'S BEEN DOWN THERE FOREVER! ISN'T IT TIME FOR A SHIFT CHANGE?

FORGET IT, THERE'S NO WAY I'M SENDING YOU DOWN THERE.

BUT LEXIE, WHERE'S YOUR SENSE OF FUN?

Unwilling to send the Clown Prince of Crime to watch after Batman, Luthor sends Ultra-Humanite to relieve Cheetah. As soon as the great white ape leaves, Luthor manages to unlock the Utility Belt. Batman's gizmos and gadgets come tumbling out.

FINALLY!

WHAT ARE YOU LOOKING FOR? CAR KEYS? BREATH MINTS?

Ever the curious clown, the Joker picks up a Batarang and throws it. The razor-edged weapon embeds itself in a nearby crate. Then it explodes.

Lex Luthor continues his search until he finds Batman's passkey. The high-tech device will grant access to the Justice League Watchtower.

Like Green Lantern, Star Sapphire can use her power ring to form powerful shapes and weapons out of light.

Soon after, the Injustice League puts Lex Luthor's sinister scheme into action. Star Sapphire carries Solomon Grundy and the Shade through outer space toward the Watchtower in a protective, pink force field. Grundy is holding a special gift created just for the Justice League.

Star Sapphire's real name is Carol Ferris, CEO of Ferris Aircraft.

The villains pull up outside the Watchtower's docking bay and the Shade activates Batman's passkey. BEEP BOOP BEEP. Upon entering, a silent alarm notifies Martian Manhunter that there has been an unlawful entry.

Suddenly, the hero from Mars is swarmed by darkness! Martian Manhunter is ambushed by a night-vision-goggled Solomon Grundy and knocked unconscious.

WHOOSH!

Back at the prison, the rest of the team gathers for a status report. Superman informs them that Copperhead is of no help. Wonder Woman's communicator alerts the team that there is trouble at the Watchtower.

MARTIAN MANHUNTER SOUNDED THE ALARM!

THEN WHAT ARE WE WAITING FOR? LET'S GET UP THERE!

Meanwhile, the Joker pulls up a TV in front of Batman so he can watch the Injustice League's terrible plot unfold in real time. He even brought popcorn along for the occasion.

IT'S SHOW TIME, BATSIE! THERE'S A SURPRISE HIDDEN IN YOUR LITTLE CLUBHOUSE. AND ONCE YOUR CHUMS GET THERE, KA-BLOOEY!

The Clown Prince of Crime cackles at his own joke and then offers the Dark Knight some of his snack. Batman ignores him.

POPCORN? OH, WELL. MORE FOR ME.

Upset with the Joker's sick sense of humor, Ultra-Humanite gets up and leaves the room. The criminal clown laments the loss of another spectator, but he relishes being alone with his arch nemesis. It allows the Joker time to mess with Batman's mind.

Aside from menacing Gotham City, the Joker's only goal is to defeat Batman once and for all!

JOKER, YOU NAUSEATE ME.

AWW. THE BIG GALOOT IS GOING TO MISS THE SHOW—AND THE SEQUEL!

WHAT'S THE SEQUEL?

AFTER THE BOMB GETS YOUR FRIENDS, I GET YOU. HAHAHA!

Martian Manhunter's powers include flight, invisibility, extreme strength, laser vision, shape-shifting, and telepathy!

The Justice League travels through space in their shuttle, the Javelin 7. Once they touch down, The Flash is the first to zoom out of the aircraft. He rushes to Martian Manhunter's side.

J'ONN, SPEAK TO ME.

I'LL TAKE HIM TO THE MEDICAL BAY. YOU GO FIND BATMAN!

All of those powers come with one major drawback: J'onn has a severe weakness to fire.

From its hidden location, the package Solomon Grundy left behind blinks steadily as its explosive contents count down to ignition.

52

In the medical bay, Superman, The Flash, and Wonder Woman observe Martian Manhunter's condition. Green Lantern and Hawkgirl fly in after their search.

His favorite snack is chocolate cookies.

WE CAN'T FIND BATMAN ANYWHERE.

BREEP BREEP! The Justice League gets a call and Wonder Woman answers.

THERE'S A WHAT? WHERE! HELLO?

IT WAS AN ANONYMOUS CALLER. HE SAYS THERE'S A BOMB UP HERE.

The Justice League immediately springs into action. They split up in different directions with hopes of covering more ground before it is too late!

53

Wonder Woman and The Flash search the main floor. The Flash zigs and zags and zooms through the landing and control panel. Wonder Woman lifts an enormous generator off the ground and looks underneath.

NOT HERE.

NOPE.

NADA.

ZILCH.

Hawkgirl and Superman soar overhead, making an aerial sweep of the higher reaches of the Watchtower. Superman uses his X-ray vision to see through the walls.

UPPER LEVELS ARE CLEAR!

NOTHING ON THIS DECK, EITHER.

Green Lantern uses his power ring to create an energy beam flashlight. Soon he discovers a set of mysterious footprints. He follows them and eventually comes upon the dangerous device.

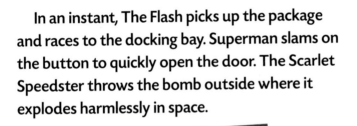

I'VE PICKED UP A FAINT THERMAL PATTERN. FLASH! OVER HERE!

In an instant, The Flash picks up the package and races to the docking bay. Superman slams on the button to quickly open the door. The Scarlet Speedster throws the bomb outside where it explodes harmlessly in space.

KA-BOOM!

In their secret lair, the Injustice League gathers around a monitor as they await the detonation of the bomb. Lex Luthor witnesses the explosion and jumps for joy. When the smoke clears, the evil genius learns that the Watchtower is still standing. Meaning, the Justice League survived! He goes into a frenzy and throws his chair into the television.

NO! THEY SHOULD BE COSMIC DUST!

SMASH!

Back at the Watchtower, Hawkgirl tries to reach Batman, but the Dark Knight is still not answering his communicator. Martian Manhunter begins to stir. When the hero is fully alert, he informs his teammates about the events that transpired.

The Justice League comes to the realization that their friend is in dire danger if he is in the clutches of the Injustice League. They quickly come up with a plan to find him.

Luther's genius mind anticipated Batman contacting Martian Manhunter with telepathy, so he locked Batman in a stasis cell.

The Joker is unhappy that the Injustice League's little prank was not successful. Then the jester jeers and menaces Batman with an old-fashioned, yet still effective, weapon.

HOW CLOSE DO YOU LIKE YOUR SHAVE?

THIS CLOSE.

CLUNK!

NOT FAIR, BATMAN!

Unfortunately for Luthor, Solomon Grundy is much more easily outwitted.

Batman hits the Joker with his armor-plated cowl. The Clown Prince of Crime drops his weapon and falls onto his behind. Both his top and bottom are as bruised as his ego. Rushing at Batman to deliver a killing blow, the Joker is suddenly restrained by Solomon Grundy.

58

The Joker storms out of the room. Batman knows that the simpleminded Grundy could be the key to his escape.

Water often destroys electrical devices, which is why it's important not to get them wet!

Grundy complies and returns with Batman's water. He even helps the Caped Crusader take a sip. Without warning, Batman spits the liquid up into the electric control panel stasis cell. The device shorts out in a shower of sparks and smoke. Batman immediately contacts Martian Manhunter with his mind.

Upstairs, Lex Luthor almost collapses from fatigue. Ultra-Humanite helps him into a chair but Luthor refuses to admit that he is weak.

I CAN'T GIVE UP NOW. I NEED TO BUY MORE TIME.

I CAN HELP YOU, BUT IT WILL COST EXTRA.

WHIRRRRR!

THIS CONTAINMENT UNIT SHOULD STABILIZE YOUR CONDITION.

The villains all meet in the lab, where Ultra-Humanite has made some alterations to Luthor's machines. The great ape scientist rushes from panel to panel, turning knobs and shifting gears. The machinery hums to life with extra power.

Humanite rigs Luthor up to the machine and begins his experiment. The table glows and sparks with electricity. Luthor is encased in a field of glowing energy and soon fitted with a custom-made chest plate that fuses to his body. The other villains look on in suspense as Luthor howls in pain. Then there is silence.

A traitor is someone who goes behind his or her allies' backs to aid the enemy!

Suddenly, Solomon Grundy comes running up from the basement and stumbles into the lab.

MR. LUTHOR! MR. LUTHOR! BATMAN *GOT OUT OF* THAT THINGIE!

OUR FIRST ORDER OF BUSINESS IS TO DISCOVER THE TRAITOR.

TRAITOR?!

The leader of the Injustice League turns on the surveillance footage. An array of different camera views pops onto the large computer screen. Before he can rewind the tape, Luthor's attention is diverted elsewhere.

All together, the villains witness Martian Manhunter phasing through the wall in his intangible state. Luthor orders Ultra-Humanite to seize the intruder.

One of Martian Manhunter's powers is intangibility, or the ability to move through solid objects.

THE ONLY WAY THE JUSTICE LEAGUE COULD HAVE FOUND THAT BOMB IS IF ONE OF US TOLD THEM!

Down in the basement, Ultra-Humanite waits for Martian Manhunter to make his entrance. Just as the hero enters to save his friend, the mad scientist attacks.

Ultra-Humanite impales Martian Manhunter's phased form with an electrical rod that converts him back into a solid state and knocks him out.

GRRRRRR!

ZAP!

07:02.000
BASEMENT
CAM 1 ▶ ▶ ▶

SO MUCH FOR BEING STEALTHY.

Unfortunately, his intangible form is still vulnerable to electrical attacks.

Hawkgirl is known for her strength and bravery, not her patience or subtlety.

Across the street from the Injustice League's hideout, the Justice League awaits contact from Martian Manhunter. Several minutes pass and they grow very concerned. Hawkgirl is itching to get inside and help her friends.

HE'S BEEN IN THERE TOO LONG.

SOMETHING'S WRONG.

While bats are often called "flying rodents," they're actually mammals of the order Chiroptera, which comes from the Greek words for "hand" and "wing."

Hawkgirl leads the charge and smashes through the front entrance with her mace. BASH! The Flash zooms in right behind her. Superman breaks a hole through the wall as Green Lantern crashes in through the window. SMASH! CRASH!

WE SURE KNOW HOW TO MAKE AN ENTRANCE!

The Justice League finds their adversaries waiting for them. Solomon Grundy, Star Sapphire, the Joker, and the Shade are ready for battle.

> IT APPEARS WE HAVE OURSELVES SOME UNINVITED GUESTS.

> PESTS, IS MORE LIKE IT. AS IF THE FLYING RODENT IN THE BASEMENT WASN'T BAD ENOUGH...

> AND YOU'LL BE MAKING A QUICK EXIT, TOO!

Without further ado, the Justice League strikes! Green Lantern shoots a beam of hard light energy at their adversaries, but it is deflected by Star Sapphire's luminous force field.

The largest known species of bat can grow to have a wingspan of more than five and a half feet!

ZAP!

The living zombie charges at the super heroes. Superman zooms toward Grundy, hitting him with a force more powerful than a locomotive. They blast through a wall into another storage room, and crash against a large concrete staircase.

BAM!

WHAP!

WHAP!

POW!

Solomon Grundy is back on his feet and takes a swing at Superman. The man of steel easily evades the monster's massive fist and returns with two rapid jabs and a swift right hook.

Grundy sails into the large plaster statue of a cartoon duck. The zombie recovers and gets an idea! He lifts the statue high over his head and hurls it at Superman. Superman punches the statue in two with a thunderous uppercut.

The tail of the duck lands on top of Grundy, pinning him to the ground.

Superman splits his time between Metropolis and his Fortress of Solitude, which is hidden deep in the Arctic. It has artifacts from his home planet.

GRUNDY DESTROY THE JUSTICE LEAGUE!

Before becoming a member of the Green Lantern Corps, John Stewart was a proud United States Marine.

The Justice League follows Superman's lead into the fray. Hawkgirl and The Flash attack first, but Star Sapphire fires a beam of cosmic energy, knocking The Flash off balance. He tumbles onto Hawkgirl and they fall backward.

> THAT'S NOT THE FIRST TIME I'VE SWEPT A MAN OFF HIS FEET.

Green Lantern intercepts Star Sapphire's next blast with one of his own, causing hers to fizzle like stardust.

Star Sapphire soars into the air and matches Green Lantern blow for blow. The luminous battle lights up the dark warehouse with flashes of magenta and green. The opponents seem to be evenly matched.

Green Lantern looks far in the distance
and sees Superman lift something into the air.
He makes a quick joke while Star Sapphire
draws closer.

At that moment, the other half of the cartoon
mascot hurtles through the air and brains Star
Sapphire. The villainess crumples to the floor in
an unconscious heap.

In addition
to creating
powerful
energy
constructs,
John's ring
also serves as
a universal
translator
and a
navigation
device when
traveling
through
space.

Hawkgirl charges her mace and swoops down at Shade. He dives for cover, and Hawkgirl narrowly misses her target. She soars back up and around, diving toward the villain again.

OUR TEAM IS FALLING APART!

AND YOU'LL BE THE NEXT TO FALL, SHADE.

LOOKS LIKE LITTLE BIRDIE GOT HER WINGS CLIPPED.

This time, the shady villain is faster than the flying hero. He aims his nightstick and shoots a concentrated dose of living darkness at Hawkgirl. Shrouded in the thick substance, the winged warrior loses control and crashes into two statues.

The Joker sees Wonder Woman flying toward him. He knows he is no match for the amazing Amazon and turns tail. She snares him in her lasso, pinning his arms down. The crafty prankster pulls out a baby doll and lobs it at Wonder Woman.

Wonder Woman is momentarily distracted by the toy. Suddenly, it explodes, sending the Amazon princess flying across the room.

The Joker laughs with glee and runs away. The Shade decides that is a good idea and turns to make his escape—but his path is blocked by The Flash! The Flash punches the fleeing foe right in the face. The Shade drops his nightstick and Hawkgirl snatches it up.

GIVE ME THAT!

YOU DON'T KNOW HOW TO USE IT!

YEAH, I DO.

Hawkgirl swings the nightstick, delivering a sucker punch right to the Shade's gut. Then she knocks him to the ground. Another member of the Injustice League is down for the count.

The Flash spies the Joker making a run for it and rushes toward him.

The jeering jester pulls out his exploding marbles and drops them on the ground. They roll under the Scarlet Speedster's rapidly moving feet. He stumbles and gets lifted into the air by their detonation.

I STILL HAVE SOME MORE TRICKS UP MY SLEEVES!

BLAM!

YOU GET POINTS FOR STYLE, BUT YOUR LANDING IS A BIT OFF.

Luthor is willing to sacrifice almost anything to defeat Superman...

The Joker runs down into the basement to settle his score with the Caped Crusader–but Batman is missing! Furious, the madman searches the basement until he comes face-to-face with his formidable foe.

Enraged, the Joker throws a punch at Batman, but the Dark Knight grabs his fist. Batman wipes the smile off the Joker's face with a knockout punch.

With the fight winding down, Superman flies over to Solomon Grundy, the only remaining conscious member of the Injustice League.

The Man of Steel is blasted off his feet by two intense energy beams. Lex Luthor appears with an advanced suit of armor—one that is fueled by Kryptonite!

...but Superman won't let evil triumph without a fight!

Superman and Lex Luthor continue their sensational showdown. Superman punches his opponent, but his super-strength is quickly diminishing. Luthor barrages Superman with a concentrated dose of Kryptonite rays. The Man of Steel struggles against the energy-sucking attack but grows weaker by the second.

Just as Luthor is about to achieve his ultimate victory, Ultra-Humanite jabs him in the back with his electrical rod! Luthor's armor overloads from the high voltage charge and shuts down.

The Justice League rushes to Superman's side, prompting Ultra-Humanite to raise his hands and surrender. He was the traitor all along! Superman's strength slowly returns and the battle is now over. The Justice League has won.

Soon after, the Metropolis police force arrives with heavy artillery and armored trucks to cart the villains away. The Injustice League has been dismantled once and for all. As he is led away in bonds, Ultra-Humanite stops to talk to Batman.

That night, Lex Luthor and Ultra-Humanite are back in their neighboring prison cells. And, just like his last visit, Luthor is again aggravated by the unbearable classical opera that the Humanite is playing at a very high volume. He pounds his fists against the wall.

Ultra-Humanite is very pleased with this turn of events. He is comfortable in his cell, enjoying the performance through to its completion. More enjoyable, of course, is that it annoys Lex Luthor to no end.

Lex Luthor tried to defeat the Justice League by creating his own team of super powered individuals—the Injustice League. That team, however, lacked many of the terrific traits that make the Justice League such a formidable force. This great team stands for honor, loyalty, and, above all, friendship. United, they are unstoppable and together, the Justice League always saves the day!

Every member of the Justice League is strong, but the League's greatest strength is teamwork!